MR. CHRISTA

by Roger Hargreaves

Illustrated by
Adam Hargreaves

MR.MEN **LITTLE MISS**

MR. MEN and LITTLE MISS™ & © The Hargreaves Organisation

PRICE STERN SLOAN

ISBN 0-8431-2110-6   1 0 9 8 7 6 5 4 3 2 1

In my snow-covered cottage at the South Pole
I was having breakfast.

That frosty morning, as I was popping the last
piece of marmalade-covered plum pudding into
my mouth, there was a knock on the door of
Mistletoe Cottage.

When I opened the door, I saw that it was
the mailman.

"Hello, Percy," I said. "Come on in out of the cold."

"I've got a letter for you," said Percy. "And as it has a North Pole postmark, I suppose it's from your uncle."

Everybody at the South Pole knows about my famous uncle who lives at the North Pole.

"Good old Santa Claus," I chuckled. "Haven't heard from him in ages!"

"Well," remarked Percy, "thanks for the warm-up. I had better be off now."

I opened the envelope.

"Dear Nephew," read the letter, "I hope all is well down there. We are busy as usual up here, getting things organized for Christmas. Which is one of the reasons I am writing to you.

"Can you help?

"Each year I am finding it more and more difficult to get around to all those Mr. Men! There seem to be so many of them all over the place, and I was wondering if, this year, as a big favor to your old uncle, you could stand in for me?

"Hoping you can help. Your ever loving uncle."

That very evening I put through a long distance call to the North Pole.

"Hello?" chuckled a rather deep, rumbly voice at the other end of the telephone. "Santa Claus speaking!"

"Hello, Uncle," I said. "Your letter arrived this morning, and I'd love to help!"

"Oh, good for you," the voice rumbled in my ear. "If you have a pencil and paper, I'll give you the Mr. Men's names and addresses. I'll lend you a couple of reindeer if you like."

"Oh no," I said. "I can manage."

I read through the list of Mr. Men while I was having supper.

"First things first," I thought to myself. "And the first thing I need is transport!"

"And the first thing to do if I need transport," I thought as I chewed, "is to talk to Wizard Winterbottom!"

The following morning, I set off to see the Wizard.

I was quite out of breath by the time I arrived at Wizard Winterbottom's castle.

I must say Wizard Winterbottom's castle is the biggest castle I've ever seen.

Mind you, it has to be big, because Wizard Winterbottom is a giant.

"Christmas!" Wizard Winterbottom boomed in a voice that made my head spin. "How nice to see you! Come in!"

"Now," thundered Wizard Winterbottom. "What brings you here on a cold winter's morning like this?"

I told him all about my famous uncle, and all about how I'd been asked for help, and all about the Mr. Men, and all about where they lived, and all about the fact that I needed transport. Special transport!

"Can you help me?" I asked hopefully.

"Yes," he said eventually. "But I can't do anything until the middle of next week!"

"Thank you very much," I replied.

"Goodbye!" I shouted, but he didn't hear me. He was already too busy thinking.

Exactly two weeks later I paid a return visit to the enormous castle.

He took me into his kitchen, lifted me up onto his enormous table, and set me down with a bit of a bump.

"There's your transport," said Wizard Winterbottom.

"But that's your teapot!" I said in bewilderment.

"You've heard of flying saucers," he laughed. "Well, you're looking at the world's first flying teapot!"

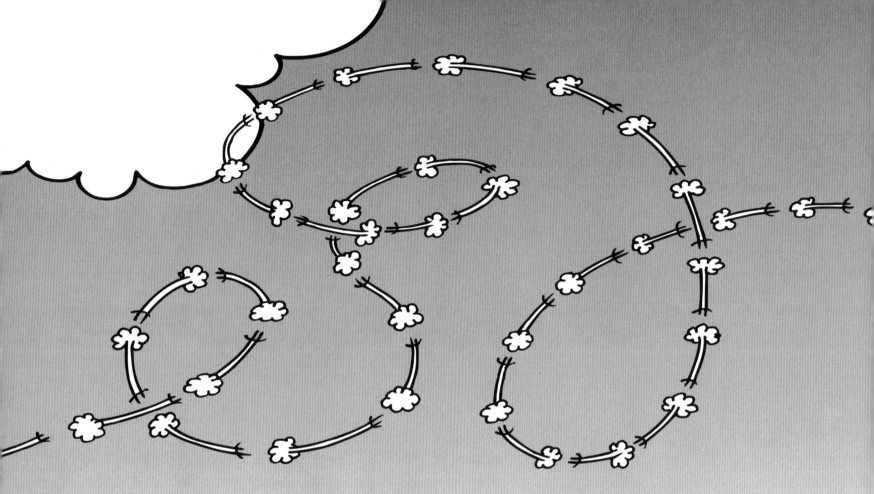

We took the Flying Teapot outside the castle, and
I pressed the start button in great excitement.

I zoomed right around the South Pole in no time at all
and landed safely back at the castle.

"Well?" asked Wizard Winterbottom.

I was at a loss for words.

"Fanjollytastic?" suggested the wizard.

I grinned. "Absojollylutely," I replied.

That evening, I sat down and made a list of Christmas presents for all the Mr. Men.

A very long list.

I didn't finish until three o'clock in the morning!

I spent the next week and a half wrapping up all the presents, and almost before I knew it, December 24th arrived.

Christmas Eve!

"It's going to be a long day," I thought to myself as I packed all the brightly-colored parcels into my Flying Teapot.

It was snowing lightly as I took off from the South Pole.

That Christmas Eve was indeed a very long day, and a very long night, too.

And the moon was just disappearing over the horizon of Loudland when I delivered the last of the presents to Mr. Quiet.

I was quite exhausted.

Christmas morning dawned, and all over the world everyone started to open their presents.

At seven o'clock Mr. Fussy opened his present. Three hundred and sixty-five yellow housecoats. One for every day of the year!

At five past seven Mr. Small opened his present. One jelly bean! Gift wrapped. Banana flavored. A feast!

At ten past seven Mr. Greedy opened his present. A cookbook entitled *1001 Ways to Roast an Ox!* Mr. Greedy licked his lips and rubbed his tummy.

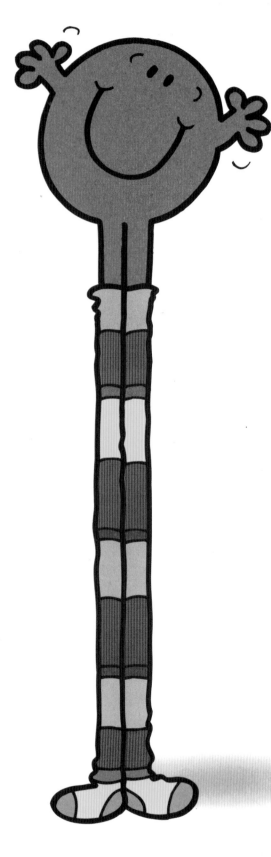

At quarter past seven Mr. Tall opened his present. Socks. Striped socks. The longest, stripiest pair of stretchy socks you've ever seen!

At twenty past seven Mr. Muddle opened a packet of cornflakes. "Funny sort of present," he thought to himself, not noticing his real present.

At twenty-five past seven Mr. Mean opened his present. A purse. A very, very small purse. Just small enough not to hold any money!

At half past seven Mr. Forgetful opened his present. "Is it my birthday?" he thought to himself.

At twenty to eight Mr. Chatterbox opened his present. A dictionary. "How very very very very very very very very useful," he murmured.

At quarter to eight Mr. Topsy-Turvy opened his present. A picture. "How nice," he said as he hung it on the wall. Upside down!

At ten to eight Mr. Uppity opened his present. A present for the man who has everything. A gold-plated backscratcher!

At five to eight Mr. Funny opened his present. A book of knock-knock jokes. Knock knock! Who's there? You know the sort of thing.

And, at eight o'clock precisely, Mr. Silly opened his present. An electric, fully automatic, instant, digital, computerized Thingumajig?

I've no idea!

Just after eight o'clock that Christmas morning the telephone rang.

"Hello," rumbled a voice.

"Hello," I answered. "Merry Christmas!"

"And a Merry Christmas to you, too. How did it go?" Santa Claus asked me.

"Just got back," I said.

"Me too," sighed my uncle wearily. "I had a bit of a problem in France," he added. "Got stuck in a chimney."

"It's all those mince pies," I chuckled.

And that is the end of my story.

Well.

Nearly.

Almost.

Not quite.

At five o'clock in the afternoon Mr. Slow finally managed to open his present.

Five o'clock in the afternoon was the time.

And the day?

New Year's Eve!

MR. MEN

Mr. Tickle   Mr. Greedy   Mr. Happy   Mr. Nosey   Mr. Sneeze   Mr. Bump   Mr. Snow   Mr. Messy   Mr. Topsy-Turvy   Mr. Silly

Mr. Uppity   Mr. Small   Mr. Daydream   Mr. Forgetful   Mr. Jelly   Mr. Noisy   Mr. Lazy   Mr. Funny   Mr. Mean   Mr. Chatterbox

Mr. Fussy   Mr. Bounce   Mr. Muddle   Mr. Dizzy   Mr. Impossible   Mr. Strong

Mr. Grumpy   Mr. Clumsy   Mr. Quiet   Mr. Rush   Mr. Tall   Mr. Worry   Mr. Nonsense   Mr. Wrong   Mr. Skinny   Mr. Mischief

Mr. Clever   Mr. Busy   Mr. Slow   Mr. Brave   Mr. Grumble   Mr. Perfect   Mr. Cheerful   Mr. Cool   Mr. Rude   Mr. Good